who could love an ugly toad?

Story and Illustrations

by

NORMA
BRISTOL
FISCHER

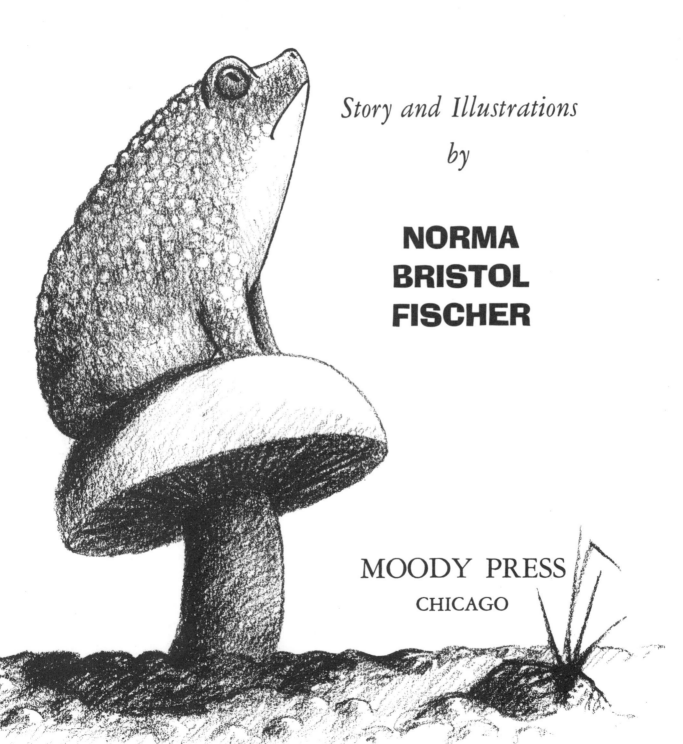

MOODY PRESS

CHICAGO

Printed in the United States of America

For

Christopher, Lara, and Andre

"Ha, ha, ha," laughed the salamanders.

"Look at that **ugly** toad!"

Gertrude crawled away, embarrassed.

Gertrude looked at her face in the water.

"Oh why, oh why did God make me so ugly-looking?" she moaned. "Every time I look at myself, I feel all **ugly** inside. It ruins my whole day!

"Nobody loves me. *Crrr-o-a-k.*"

I'll just go jump into a mud puddle and forget about to-day, she thought.

She hopped away toward her favorite mudhole.

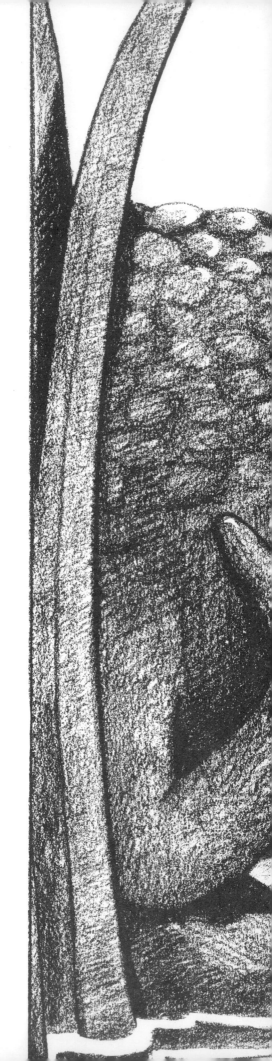

"One more, one more, one more piece of grass. One more, and my home will be finished," trilled Mr. Marsh Wren.

But just then, Gertrude came hopping through the grass. She was so unhappy, she didn't even watch where she was going.

CRASH! She kicked a big hole in the side of the nest.

Mr. Wren was so upset, he dropped the grass he was carrying. "My poor, poor, poor, poor house!" he cried. But Gertrude said nothing to him. She just hopped away, mumbling, "Nobody loves me. *Crrr-o-a-k!* Nobody loves me."

Suddenly she came upon her friend Tilly Turtle.

Tilly was asleep on her favorite rock, sunning herself. She was right in the middle of the path, but Gertrude didn't stop. She jumped right on top of her to the next rock.

SPLASH! Tilly was thrown into the water.

But Gertrude didn't even look around.

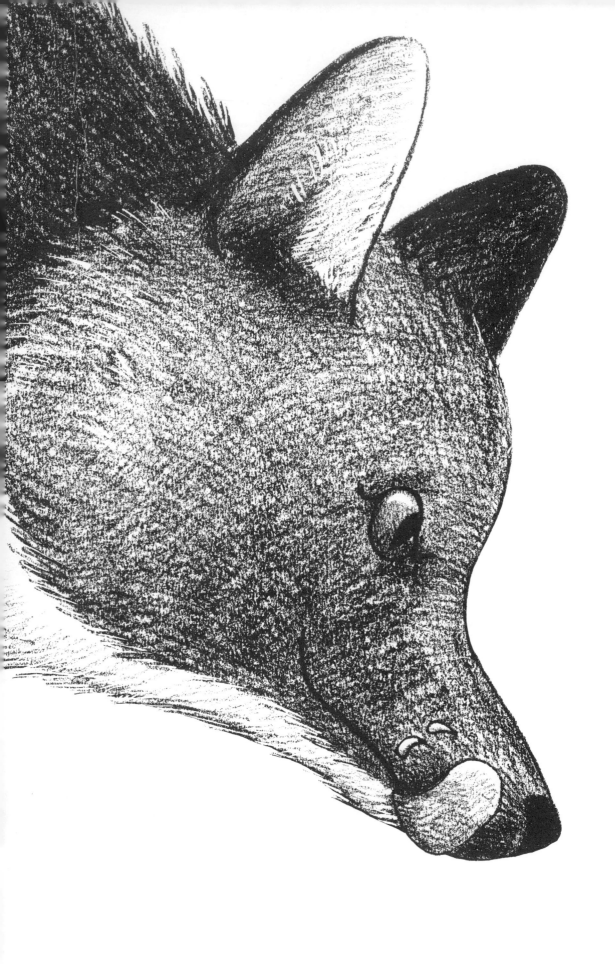

Gertrude had almost reached her puddle, when a big, hungry fox came running across her path. He saw her hopping along and said, "Aha! I see a delicious toad for my dinner!"

"Heh-heh!"

The fox looked again and couldn't see Gertrude anywhere. "Where did she go?" he asked with surprise. "I know I saw a toad just a moment ago. Where did she go?" He blinked his eyes. "I'm sure I saw a toad. I know I did."

"Oh well," he said sadly, "I'll find something else to eat." And off he went down the path.

Can you see Gertrude?

When she was sure the fox wasn't coming back, Gertrude hopped over into the grass and sat there. She closed her eyes and took a deep breath. The grass and earth and flowers seemed to smell sweeter than ever before. A soft wind blew, and birds were singing.

She opened her eyes and looked around her. Never had the flowers looked so pretty.

Gertrude looked down at the damp, brown, bumpy earth. Never had it looked so beautiful.

"Why," she exclaimed, "I look just like the earth! *Crr-o-a-k!* I'm brown and bumpy and **beautiful**, too. I can hardly see myself against the ground.

"No wonder the fox couldn't find me!"

"God must love me very much to make me so **beautiful**. *Crrr-o-a-k*"! she cried out loud. The more she thought about God's great love for her, the happier she felt. She felt so good inside, she did a little dance for joy, thanking God for her life in this beautiful world.

Then Gertrude remembered what she
had done to her friends.
That made her sad again.
So she decided she had
better go to see them.

Gertrude found Mr. Wren first.
"I'm sorry for the mess I made,"
she said, as she helped the
little wren gather grass.
While they worked, Gertrude
told him why she had been upset.
"I had just seen my reflection
in the water and thought I was
ugly-looking. I became angry with
God for making me that way.
I was mad at everything; so when
your house was in the way, I kicked it.

"I hope you will forgive me."

"I forgive, forgive, forgive you," Mr.
Wren replied. *"Cheerie, cheerie,
cheerie!* What cheered you up?"

Gertrude told him how the fox almost ate her up. "But," she cried,
"he couldn't find me. I looked just
like the ground. And you know what!
God made me look like the earth to
hide me from my enemies.

Oh, that
makes me
so happy!"

Tilly Turtle was glad to see her good friend. "You really didn't hurt me when you knocked me into the water; you just surprised me." The turtle heard Gertrude's story and was happy for her. That made her think for a moment, then she said, "God takes care of me too!"

"Oh?" replied Gertrude.

"Yes! Watch!"

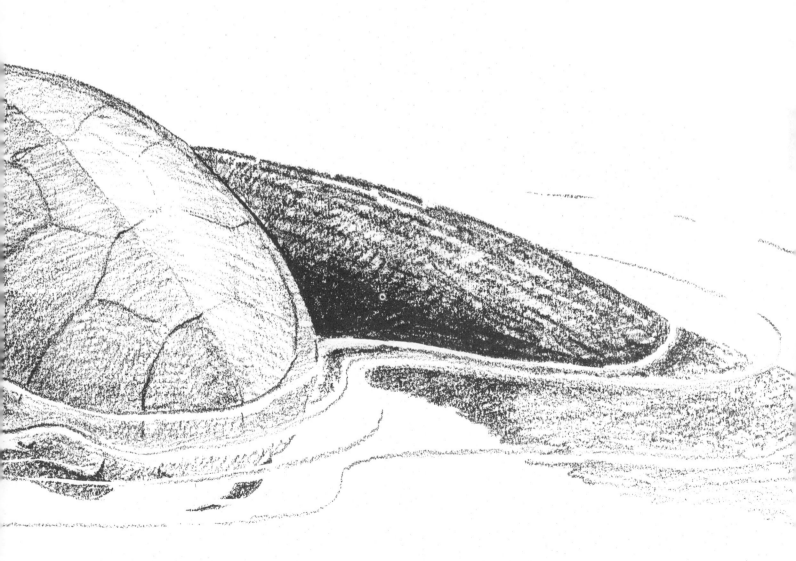

"Where did you go? Where did you go?" cried Gertrude.

"Nobody can eat **me** up." The turtle laughed from inside her shell. "A nasty old fox tried to one day, but he finally gave up." They both chuckled.

Gertrude was still laughing as she hopped her
way home in the late afternoon.

That night, Gertrude croaked happily in the light of the full moon. Over and over she sang, "God loves me and protects me. God loved me enough to make me brown and bumpy and beautiful. *Crrrrr-o-a-k!* Brown and bumpy and beautiful, just like the earth." Deep down inside, the little toad felt warm and loved and **beautiful**.